STREAMS OF GIFT

BIBEK AARUNYA KAFLE

Copyright © Bibek Aarunya Kafle
All Rights Reserved.

Bibek Aarunya Kafle

A river of blood flowed in Beni, peace messenger come here and build
a huge dam.

Contents

Foreword

Hey don't skip

Nepal passed through a decade long (1996- 2006) violent conflict as a consequence of which Nepali people suffered severe threats to their state of political, social, economic, psychological and physical well being. The year 1996 marked the beginning of the armed conflict as the Communist Party of Nepal (Maoist) [CPN (Maoist)] launched the 'People's War' against the state. The CPN (Maoist) submitted a 40-point demand to the Government of Nepal (GoN) on 4 February 1996 and had threatened if their demands were not met by 17 February, they would start armed struggle. However, the 'People's War' was declared 4 days before the actual deadline they had given to the government. As stated in their documents of the time, the aim of launching armed struggle in Nepal was to establish a 'new people's democracy' (similar to China in 1949)', under the leadership of them which was also called in their terminology as 'dictatorship of proletariat' through protracted guerrilla war by overthrowing the multi-party democratic system which was established in 1990 after the popular mass uprising. The newly established multi-party democratic governments at the time were about to institutionalize democratic system and also address the long pending social and economic problems of the country. However, due to the intra-party and inter-party conflicts and frequent changes of the government, the successive elected governments failed to address those burning issues that led to frustration and disappointment among the common people. The inter-party squabbles, political instability and failure to address the common people's expectations in the post 1990s democracy provided fertile ground to the extreme forces like the CPN (Maoist) to assert their agendas and escalate violent activities. They were able to capitalize the prevailing pathetic political and social situation of the time and quickly expand their influence and activities throughout the country. Hence, the country entered into protracted conflict that took ten years to resolve and endured a high human and socio-economic cost. The armed conflict caused large number of deaths, disappearances, dislocation, displacement, violence, damages of property and infrastructure along with economic down turns.

Preface

Beni Bazar lies in the Myagdi district headquarter. This lies at an altitude of 899 meters above sea level. It stands at the intersection of two rivers, the river Kali Gandaki and the river Myagdi. It is 12 km from Baglung and about 300 km from Kathmandu to the west. It has become a major tourist attraction and accommodation in the Annapurna circuit. Getting to Beni takes 9-10 hours by bus drive from Kathmandu.

The 2004 Beni attack was one of the biggest attacks by the People's liberation army (PLA) of Communist part of Nepal, Maoist, during the Nepalese civil war(1996–2006). Almost the entire western division of the PLA, numbering around 3,500, attacked government positions in Beni, the district headquarters of Myagdi district in western Nepal, on 20 March 2004 at around 10 PM. Hundreds of civilians were used for logistics. Around 90 soldiers of the PLA and dozens of police and military personnel as well as civilians died. Multiple government buildings were destroyed and dozens of members of the civil service and government forces were kidnapped by the PLA.

Acknowledgements

As I always tried to understand this fact of history, my soul searched for this story. The story of an ordinary man who has been close to Beni throughout his life. The story reveals the village life around Beni. Story reveals the scene before the attack on Beni and the events after it. Before starting, it is better to know background knowledge, So I wrote this long information for you. You need to know that some words in the story belongs to specific nepalese names, places names, god names and many more typical. I am greatfut to my parents, friends and god for this success in writing such story.

This Book is for my readers who always love me, believe in me and encourage me to write more.

You can comment and give feedback to this book in my E-mail (bibekaarunya@gmail.com). My contact number is +977 9869111072. I am available anytime for good and bad reviews.

Prologue

This book is sold subject to the condition that it shall not, by way of trade or otherwise, be lent, resold, hired out, or otherwise circulated without publisher's prior consent in any form of binding or cover other than that in which it is published and without a similar condition including this condition being imposed on the subsequent purchaser.

CHAPTER ONE

Depth of the sky

*What kind of auspicious sign of nature is this? Why is the sun rise's beginning is soo beautiful today? How bright is the world even without starting the day with the light of the bright sun? Although, **Dassain** festival has already arrived in the courtyard and the arrival of foreign guests to everyone's house, This world is so bright today because of the glow on the faces of those villager. Otherwise, the village houses would be lit only by the powerful rays of the sun. Nowadays, there is a lamp that illuminates even the absolute darkness of the night, but nowadays I see even more darkness in the village. There is nothing wrong with nature, nature has created everything beautiful. If our sons and brothers were together, how bright it would have been even if this **Banshkharka** village was located in desert.*

This feeling towards the lonely village will always be imagined in my mind, even today. My village, full of foreigners, was really bright when I was sitting in the yard facing the eastern sun with an old, small and round dressed up mirror and a pair of tweezers in my hand. Bringing joy to the eyes, I picked up the mirror with my left hand and put my face in front of it and I was suddenly fed up with myself. Like marigold and mums blooming all over the village, my mustache has also blossomed, being dense white. One mind, when the flower blooms, it is happy and when the beard, hair blooms, it hurts. Flowering is the beginning of a new life, but after forty-seven years, what kind of mine life is yet to begin ? Rather, it is better to change the language, the hairs of my mustache are not blooming, they are withered, Just as a tired flower plant wilts towards the end. While looking in the mirror, the whitened and gray hairs are being pulled out one by one by the squeezer, and I realize that I am getting old. Realization that the body that can be enjoyed only once should be enjoyed in many ways. Seeing my mirror image reflected in the flickering mirror, I threw a pinch on the ground and stopped. After all, for whom am I trying to maintain a youthful appearance? Do progressive time stopped in plucking withered hair? After all, what is the purpose of this work? Leaving the mirror on the ground, I disappeared into the depths of the sky.

• 3 •

CHAPTER TWO

Flash back to the war

When the wind blows in the middle of the night, when the storm blows,

As the rain falls under the dark blue sky,

I will come there, and I will come there.

Lorose

Some revolutionary red soldiers were attracting the villagers in **Chautara** *by singing with* **sarangi** *and* **madal** *tunes. There was no presence of the audience like in the various musical programs held in the village. However, the* **sarangi** *and* **madal** *that they filled with were as much as a gun to everyone, everyone craves even though they were full of flowers. There was only a crowd of heroes who walked* with the revolution as their main duty and liberation as their main goal, and some young people who remained in the village for the sacrifice. "Those who always carry guns are with musical instruments today, **Mabaadi** are singing good songs in school, what about going there?" The **Posta** brother and I went down with the cows, grazing on the upper spit. By the time we reached, the program was over. They were muttering to themselves, collecting foods and vegetable bags, staggered out of there with **sarangi** and **madal** which did not suit with their green dress at all. The revolutionaries came to inform the villagers that villagers should manage the grocery required for the next one month within a week and then should not go to **Beni Bazar** and its surroundings for a month. As soon as I heard this from my friends, I realise that a big attack and confrontation was being prepared, I still remember that I reached home in a few steps. I told everything in one breath to **Idhya**.

"**Idhya**" is my first life, the world I had to live without **Idhya** is my second life. I can't pinpoint the actual time when the intimate feeling of love was established between us, but **Idhya** is present in every event that happened in my life since my childhood. I don't know when I started to love **Idhya**, but **Idhya** has been in my mind *since sense of memory begins.*

I have not let the memories of playing in the dust, picking golden raspberry, biting rhododendron and returning home from school with each other's arms to fade. Perhaps the bud of love between us must have been germinated at that time when we could not understand that our existence is for each other. Even intellectual scholars have not been able to penetrate the ultimate knowledge of existence, how could our young brains understand, but in an unknown way, we have become a need for each other's daily routine. We used to play like **Radhakrishna**, *dance like* **Radhakrishna** *and fight like* **Radhakrishna**, *every moment was full of love. The moments experienced at that level of life cannot be stored in everyone's mind, why should a person remember other events from his childhood?, even he forgets that, mother fed him milk, his father took care of him, taught him to walk and picked him up when he fell. Those beautiful moments of my childhood are memorable only because they are full of* **Idhya**. *Maybe if* **Idhya** *was not there, there would be no happy memories even today. Those vague childhood memories are the first gift* **Idhya** *gave me in my life.*

*Not only that fun time is remembered, but also the incident of separation is just as fresh. **Shree Deurali Primary School** which teaches only up to class five was the reason for our separation. Reading and learning can never be completed, but at that time, **Idhya's** father felt that now **Idhya** has done with it. Not only **Idhya's** studies were missed, we missed meetings, the days were now alone, like **Radhakrishna's** separation. It was only a two and a half hour walk, but I was a child, so I had to sit and study with my uncles in **Beni**, where villager Idhya was not there. The hustle and bustle of a new place with new friends used to be different in childhood, but the memories of **Beni Bazar** are like faded without **Idhya**.*

At Beni Bazar

*While studying at **Beni Public Secondary School**, beginning was completely dedicated to studies, but the lack of **Idhya** was felt more and more with the time. Also, from time to time there were opportunities to go to village where no change was seen no matter how many times I went. The common well, road trial, streams, Forest and lovely villager are all the same but every time I used to see a change in **Idhya**. Every time I saw her, I felt that the intoxication was growing in her eyes, when her hair floated slowly in the gentle breeze, I was spread out like an ocean, her neck and chest kissed a new peak of sexuality every time, I found that her flexible waist was growing more and more. While the supernaturality of femininity was increasing inside **Idhya**, our conversation and meeting was decreasing. I didn't get a chance to play with Idhya like before, I didn't get a chance to run around in the village, I used to call when I had to call and **Idhya** would only speak for formality and disappear. Perhaps we had* *already passed that time of childhood and were embracing the beginning of youth,* **Idhya** *didn't take care of me as if she cared about growing up. When I realized that the shame that had grown up with the growing age was bothering her, I also slowly stopped calling* **Idhya** *and I stopped to go to the village from time to time. Human nature, which forgets its own person who has died, gradually put an end to that feeling that was awakened in childhood. The moaning of* **Kaligandaki** *river, the games being played in the playground at confluence of rivers, the still water of the* **Myagdi** *river, my friends and studies slowly made me feel that love towards* **Idhya** *as a lie, as a foolish mistake.* **Idhya***, who is busy in the village environment and routine, might not surely waste a moment remembering me. At a young age, I was overcome by the feeling that this feeling towards* **Idhya** *was just a passive, innocent attraction, not love, and I gradually started focusing on* **Beni's** *environment and studies.*

CHAPTER FOUR

Back to the village

*Idhya, Idhya 's memories and immature dreams were kept aside and I focused on my studies, Then I had returned to the village after a long time after completing my School Level Certificate (SLC) exam in the year 1995. It was an opportunity to forget the hustle and bustle of **Beni**, the mental pressure of studying and the challenges of exam's result and enjoy the village climate, forest greenery and solitude for a few months. Nature has made my village like heaven, the greenery here is a joy to the eyes, the ears are happy to the chirping of the birds, like this every part of me was happy. However, the beauty of the village was not enough for my eyes, my eyes were searching for something else supernatural, my ears wanted to be satisfied by hearing someone else's voice. After returning to the village, my soul, senses all searched for **Idhya** again. Even after many days of returning to the village, I did not meet with **Idhya**, that's why I was not at peace even in that happy environment. Perhaps **Idhya** was* not in the village, otherwise It is not that I did not search her. Unknowingly, while I was searching for **Idhya**, I felt my love for her again, the needs of **Idhya** when I lived in **Beni** are not false, that is true love. You can fall in love even just by remembering someone, you can get the joy of love even by embracing the memories, that's why I have been in love with **Idhya** even throughout my stay in **Beni.** It is my delusion to think that love is false when there is no physical presence, Infact **Idhya** was always with me.

❧❧❧

The arrival of spring, the nymph of seasons, added more charm to the beauty of the village. All the plants were flourishing and switching to new form, as if nature is creating a different world everywhere. It was not only the effect of spring that made it seems like the whole world was celebrating the new year, but **Idhya** was also the reason, why that new year was special. It was New Year that our sudden meeting happened after a long time in **Deurali.** "Hey! Did you not see us walking here? Why you keep that pot be upright?" My steps were suddenly stopped by the current of words that came out of **Idhya**'s bright mouth as she ascended. I also immediately returned the answer given by unconscious brain, "Are you going home of new husband? That you need well-timed." She moved from in front of me without saying a *word. Maybe she didn't say it so that other people who came along would care, otherwise she looked at me as if she will punch me. Even today, I am fanatic by her anger. My steps didn't move forward until* **Idhya** *reached far above, instead I turned back towards* **Idhya**. **Idhya** *is like the nymph of heaven described in the* **Puranas**, *her hands and arms are as white as snow, her face is like that, her eyes are so bright, her forehead is like a field, her eyes are like a border line, her lips are soft as soft leaves and her hair is like a waterfall wrapped in a red rope, her neck is full of sensuality, I was amazed by the chest and hips, the sensual steps and movements and the geometry of the whole body. Then I regretted my rude speech, I should have spoken with love to* **Idhya** *whom I met after such a long time. After* **Idhya** *disappeared from my eyes, carrying the weight of regret, I also moved towards the well to take water.*

CHAPTER FIVE

Love story

As much as my mind was busy, I was convinced that the flame of love had also appeared in **Idhya***'s heart because the meetings between us after that had convinced me. After seeing that the love magma inside the volcano would be affected even more. so, I dared to write a letter and make a proposal.* **Idhya** *was also attracted towards me from her inner heart, but she did not want to express it because she had the consciousness of love because of the femininity she got. The consciousness that love is an experience, and, experience and tolerance for the extremes of love is not as much in a man as in a woman, that's why I hastened to make a love proposal. However,* **Idhya** *continues to love even if she does not propose, perhaps that is the difference between a woman who loves and a man who loves for sensual pleasure.*

Idhya did not reply to the love letter for a long time and kept me confused because of the suddenness of my heart. **Idhya** used to speak normally as if she didn't know anything and smiled at me, at my yearning. As time passed and I started to feel that the date of that letter had passed, I was also returning to normalcy. But maybe because she understood my concern, **Idhya** used to laugh at me all the time.

God also has fixed a special day in everyone's destiny, it was the day that God had chosen for me. I asked her a question to steal her heart while we were talking, chewing sour rhododendron that had not been flourished properly.

"Your time of going on **Doli** is very near, **Idhya**" My words suddenly showed a look of disappointment on her face.

"Run away, one day it happens to everyone, What happened? How much Smart you are trying to be? **Parkashey***"*

Who's **Parkashey***? Say* **Prakash!***"*

*"***Parkashey** *is* **Parkashey***."*

*"***Pra... Ka... Sh** *is my name."*

Lorose
She took a long breath and smiled again saying **"Parkashey, parkashey, parkashey"** *in a baby soft voice.*

Immediately, intoxicated with love for many days, I embraced **Idhya***'s soft hands and pulled her towards me, she focused excitedly on my eyes and hugged me tightly like for all era. While being wrapped in her embrace, I remembered the selfless embrace with* **Idhya** *as a child, the embrace of that time was very different from the embrace of now. During my childhood, my nerves did not feel the beating of* **Idhya***'s heart like this. Maybe she was tired of our love separation and she kept her head*

*on my lap for a long time. Then I also raised her head and kissed her pink lips, which were covered in my love, she also sank deeper into the ocean of love. We are both lost in that supernatural love. Her hair was floating like a cloud in the cold breeze that came with the message of love from the mountains, In that cold moment of love, her brow was hot, **Idhya** became blowing hot air like a **loo**. Maybe the winds didn't match, suddenly she swam out of the flood of hugs, covered with shame and jumped away in excitement like a deer. **Idhya's** shame was the confession of our love. That day and that moment is the most special gift **Idhya** gave me in my life.*

Separating again

*After that, I have decorated every day in the best pages of my life spent together with **Idhya**. As in childhood, even in those days of youth, we got the chance to experience life once again. Childhood is the best dimension of life, but the secretions of youth is also the ultimate happiness of life. Life is a unity of different dimensions, nature has given us the ability to experience each dimension of time in a different way. I think that the whole enjoyment of life is to live according to the dimensional qualities, the time of stillness, the time of enjoying happiness, the time of dancing, playing and singing, the spiritual time, enjoying these parts in their entirety seems like a complete life to me. So, in those days of youth, my love lust was fulfilled and we enjoyed love and youth in full. I got to know the news of my SLC result from Idhya that makes me awake for the future while I was spending that time with **Idhya** only. There was a lot of fear on her face as she came with a flower in her hand,* *maybe she was worried about me, she loved me more than herself. "The results of the SLC have come, go Beni today! Take these holy leaves of* **Devithan** *and offer them to* **Bhagawati,** *I have vowed, do not forget!" I hurriedly took the flowers given by* **Idhya** *as her wish, without even saying good-bye to her, I reached home and informed my parents and descended to* **Beni.** *It is because* **Idhya** *vowed* **Bhagwati** *Goddess that I passed and immediately after seeing good result, I went to* **Bhagwati** *temple at confluence of rivers, I offered the promised flowers given by* **Idhya.** *At that time, many of my friends failed, but I was in the third division, which I was celebrating in my heart, while there were tears in the school. Bowing to the Goddess* **Bhagwati** *at confluence of* **Myagdi** *river and* **Kali Gandaki** *river, I remembered my mother, father, uncles and teachers who stood up for me.*

❧❧❧

There, the uncles also gave a grand welcome to me, I was very sad that I could not include my parents and **Idhya** *in that success ceremony in* **Beni.** *My heart was even more scared when my uncles informed me that they are planning to go to* **Pokhara** *tomorrow and I will also have to continue my studies there. I remembered* **Idhya** *who said goodbye to me, how happy she was to get the news that I had passed my exams, but*

I was worried that she will be broken knowing that **Prakash** *had gone to* **Pokhara** *without meeting her, but I was sure that everything was over, so I went to* **Pokhara***. I was not feeling very well in* **Pokhara** *in the state of mind saying, "she might be still waiting for me on that narrow way to* **Deurali***." I was spending my time thinking that* **Idhya** *was with me in every moment of those dark days in* **Pokhara***, while* **Idhya** *also remembered me in every moment of the village. One day, a letter was received from the village, the letter came from home, it did not mention the news of* **Idhya***. If* **Idhya** *also had sent a letter, I thought I can live on the support of that letter and was disappointed. That disappointment quickly turned into excitement, there was a letter sent by my father asking me to come home immediately. The youths of the village were going astray in the name of people's revolution, even those living in headquater city did not return to their villages and there were reports that they were joining the People's Liberation Army. At that time when there was a lack of accurate information, there was a fear that there would be riots in the country. I returned to the village thinking that it was reasonable for my father to be worried about the situation.*

success story

*The scenario of the village had changed, there was terror on the faces of the villagers, young people like me had left the village and now there were probably only a couple of us left. After I returned, both my parents were happy, but **Idhya** seems restless even when we met many times. **Idhya** used to say, "They are coming to take young people in their home, they are going to form an army to fight the government and train them to fight, you are not going to leave this village ever!" Saying that, she was wrapped in a hug and cuddled. One day she hugged me with tears in her eyes. I tried to remind **Idhya** by saying, "It's okay, I have dear **Idhya**, my father and mother in this village and why should I go anywhere." That day, **Idhya** did not accept easily, she cried until she cried a lot. Sighing "I get strong clue about my marriage" she hugged me harder and started crying. That incident came as a bigger challenge than SLC in my life, I was thinking that meeting with **Idhya**, talking to her, hugging her, kissing her* *only as love success, but a big mountain of challenges stood in front of me. However, even that mountain seemed too small for both of us, who were enjoying good love, so both of us made a mutual decision and descended to **Beni** on the same day to make long love journey a success.*

*Being well acquainted with many people in **Beni**, it was not a problem to stay overnight. Our father and mother were very scared and came to our place the next morning in search of us in the environment of preparations for the war started by the young peoples who abandoned the love of the family and followed the ideology. Our love was successful the day our family accepted our love. Our normal marriage was completed that day with mother **Bhagwati** of confluence as a witness. our relationship is already a long-term relationship, marriage was only a confession given by the society. Our parents accepted us easily, thinking that the children would be forgotten in the chaos of married life and there would be no need to follow any groups and principles. **Idhya**'s support to overcome that major challenge of life together became another major gift for me, for life.*

History of successful love is not made, but that success was historic for us. After marriage, my intimacy with **Idhya** *gave me every happiness of life.* **Idhya** *used to care about me a lot, she used to worry about me more than herself. As a river does not take its own water, as a tree does not take its fruit and as the sky does not keep the clouds gathered with itself,* **Idhya** *loved me being completely empty in herself. After doing housework, she used to help me in the field, helped me to cut grass, she took care of my food, hunger and thirst, everyone at home called* **Idhya** *has sweet hands, she took care of me and my family together, she took care of the cowshed too, even in solitude, she always engaged with me as if she was not tired from the whole day's work. She used to be equally energetic and in the end she fell asleep after leaving all the fatigue in my arms. Those moments spent with* **Idhya***gave me the knowledge that a woman's body is really powerful. Seeing all the happiness, I felt as if* **Idhya** *made our married life successful. Even in the village, I used to be happy when I heard that people talking about us, "They would not be separated, They are like a couple chosen by fate". All in all,* **Idhya** *became my inebriation, I couldn't imagine a moment without her, I have not been freed from that tightness even today.* **Idhya** *is the light of my life, her memories are the brightness that arose from it.*

Village days

"If there is to be a revolution, there must be a revolutionary party. Without the leadership of the revolutionary party, it will be difficult for the exploited classes to defeat the imperialist brokers, That's why you also have to join in building power." When we suddenly met on the way, **Sonam** *raised an irrelevant matter and I was keep looking and listening him in surprising way.*

*"What do you say is the purpose of the revolution, **Sonam**?" My reply.*

"The purpose of any revolution is reform and change."

His answer made me understand and I also replied "Okay, if there is improvement and change in the society, I will also contribute."

*"Okay, meet me tomorrow at **Chautara** with your details and this will be kept confidential."*

*No matter what **Sonam** says, I never have to keep something secret with **Idhya**. In the evening I told her the whole story while kissing **Idhya**'s soft hair wrapped in my arms. "Oh God, don't let him be like that." Saying this, she held me tightly. **Idhya**'s love cycle was so powerful that I couldn't leave her presence even if I wanted to. I am not selfish, in fact the path taken by my friends and **Sonam** was wrong for me, I also wanted change and improvement. It seemed to me that I had beloved **Idhya**, love of my parents, family, village and society which is more important than the terrible revolution that they said.*

Year 1996 February 13, **Sonam** *came to my house to meet me. "The bugle of the revolution was blown throughout the country. Today, the operations of the People's Liberation Army were successful in seven places of six districts. The government is afraid and planning to ban terrorists as insurgents. Now we will be successful soon and change in the country will be possible. I have come for the last time to ask you to join in this great work."*

There was a distinct glow on his face that day, I was also attracted to his energy, but just as he was adamant, I was adamant about my personal principles and answered him immediately.

"Revolution is not riots and violence, **Sonam,** *the kind of revolution you say will not bring change but sufferings. The country will be affected by war for a long time, even in peace after the war, it will be more difficult for the country to rise up, you are just hungry for contribution but you don't know that tomorrow when your commanders run the country, they will forget the blood and sweat of thousands like you, villages will be destroyed, and rivers*

of blood will flow, the social system will be disturbed, and the situation will be chaotic, Peace will die, I cannot support you to make the country a crisis place, Sorry."

Again he said with anger, "The religion of a warrior is to fight, this great revolution will be successful even if we have to use calmness,wealth, punishment, difference. If you are found to have done anything against us without supporting us, you will be subjected to unthinkable action." With that, he got up and disappeared with a long, long blow.

CHAPTER NINE

The next Phase

*The situation gradually changed in the village, the atmosphere of fear blew everyone's peace of mind. During that time, **Idhya** and I had many problems in our relationship too, but no matter what the situation, we did not let go away our hand from eachother. It has been twenty-seven years since the beginning of our married life, even though it has been four years since we tied the knot, our relationship has been like a nightmare since we did not have children. "Why didn't you have children until now?" There was a wave of gossip in the village. Regardless of the situation, I did not feel any change in **Idhya**'s love for me. There was not only physical but also spiritual satisfaction in our love experience, we had no complaints with each other. However, the happiness of children is also an important part of enjoying love, On top of that, women's desire for children is more distinct. Inspite of all efforts, **Idhya** was very panicked as we were not successful, her face was losing its luster due to the desire for* *children. The situation became so negative that there was a family discord at home, I was even pressured to get another marriage from home and relatives. But, I didn't need anything from* **Idhya** *and I got all the happiness that I should get from* **Idhya**. **Idhya** *used to cry infront of me in alone time and I wiped her tears saying, "I have got all the happiness from you, I don't need anyone else". She kissed my cheek with tears in her eyes, saying, "But I want a child, we should give a grandchild to our parents."* **Idhya** *also wanted me to marry someone else and have a child, but I was against everyone and took a stand not to marry again. After my parents told me that "you are backing that lady only as impotent", I understood that the importance of* **Idhya**, *who had been serving in that house for so many years, was just like an simple object. Because she is a woman, she should keep working or be discarded? So, I had given her a promise to calm* **Idhya**'s *deranged mind. Because* **Idhya** *was not like a common thing for me,* **Idhya** *occupies a special place in every part of my life. While crying I held her hand and made her promise that "as long as I live, there will be no one else in my life, it's only you." On that day* **Idhya** *cried a lot in my arms.*

There was a goss in the village, the king and the royal family were killed by the prince.

Everyone's hearts were frightened by that monotonous sound on the radio, a group of people going to king's funeral also passed through our village at that time. The nation had never faced such a crisis, there was great grief among the common people who had lost their parents. Remembering that situation, it didn't seem like any people were fighting against the king. After that incident, the whole country was feeling the lack of guardians. After that incident, the revolution, which seemed to be suppressed, added to the tumultuous atmosphere throughout the country, the attack on forty-two districts, the declaration of a state of emergency, and the clashes at **Pyuthan** *and* **Rolpa** *caused unrest everywhere. It was heard that there were initiatives for peace talks, but everyone was worried about the growing war.*

It is not that I did not get help appeal and pressure from both parties, but because of my incoherence, no one could harm me and my family. There was a dispute about whether the family should take the fallen body of brave **Abhiman** *in the bank of* **Kaligandak**i *river or whether the revolutionary group would give it a dignified funeral. The person called Comrade* **Abhiman** *is none other than my own friend* **Sonam**, *who warned me that I might be in danger a few years ago. His principled*

*personality and his energy could have been very useful to make this nation great, but today his decision has deeply hurt his family and society. At that time, I should have stopped **Sonam** by saying, "No matter who wins the war, it is the children of Nepali mothers who die, and the ones who die are the mothers' wombs, so you and I should change the way of the revolution and prepare a new organization to make change possible through the path of peace." He was not in a position to stop at that word, he was martyred in the end as he walked as the religion of a warrior. The revolutionaries couldn't stand the fight of who owns his martyred body, the revolutionaries were always troubled by the barracks of the nearby **Beni Bazar**. They had gone from that place saying that "an action that no one had thought of will take place", so the whole village bid farewell to **Sonam**'s dead body, which was won by the family. After this incident, there was a big change in the psychology of the villagers, even at home everyone understood that the childlessness of **Idhya** and I is not a big problem, but the dying humanity is a serious problem. The constant bitterness stopped, My mother used to say, "The king has been killed, **Pipalbote**'s son has been killed and thrown into the river, I don't know, what will happen to anyone else?" No, I don't want children, What will that child see after birth, "murderous violence?" born and raised child was blown up like a doll by the bullet, God please, keep peace,*

I don't need anything else." Saying heavy words full of such feelings, mother joined her hands and cried out to God. Mother's words had a lot of meaning, so Tears from everyone's eyes fell on the ground. Mother's words made us realize that the problem that we were thinking of as a problem is just an illusion, the problem is on humanity, on the country, on the people.

The worst and the best

After devaluing the democratic rights of the people, the palace took all the power in its hand and added fuel to the fire of revolution in the country. Until yesterday, the usual flickering power took the form of fire, morally and politically, the new king was sure to be weak. It was raining, the sound of screaming **Kaligandaki** *could be heard in the village, turning off the radio that was not giving any hopeful news,* **Idhya** *came near me and smiled. Yes, the country was experiencing bad days, it was going to suffer, but I could forget all the problems infront of* **Idhya**'s *smile. She pulled me and whispered something in my ear and shyly got up and went on her way. I was also delighted by her way of telling the good news, got up and danced and made a noise when I got the idea that* **Idhya** *and my sign of love is coming to this earth. It had to be shocking, after praying to many temples, gods and* *goddesses, taking many treatments, the happiness that came after the lost hope, our perfect love that was successful after eight years of marriage and It was another big gift that **Idhya** gave me.*

❧❧❧

*Some part of **Idhya**'s body was protecting and raising the sign of our love, then it became my duty to take care of her body. I stopped her from all the work that **Idhya** was occupied with and tried to keep myself busy in the service of **Idhya** and family as much as possible. I worked with all my heart and gave rest to **Idhya**, pretending to be a helper, every time she came in front of me, I used to kiss her forehead in front of everyone, and she used to run away. While the house and yard were bright with so much happiness, the situation in the country was deteriorating even more. At the same time, both sides were killed in the **Ramechhap** clash, the liberation army became more powerful and organized and attacked **Siraha** and **Rupandehi**, the imperial army colonels' houses were attacked in the capital, **Khotang, Gaighat, Janakpur, Bhaluwang, Baglung, Nepalganj** were also attacked on both sides and Many children of Nepalese people were killed. In that turbulent environment, when I was wrapped in **Idhya**'s embrace, I got all the peace, my hands were always eager to feel the heartbeat of the* child and reached to the belly of **Idhya** who was protecting our love in her belly. Sometimes I would touch with my hand for a long time and I would think, "The peace you are enjoying is not outside here. The world is very turbulent, don't be troubled by the emptiness of the world you are in, there is a troubled world outside. But you have to come, even if you come here, you have to live in peace one day, "like **Sonam**", so I am waiting for your arrival."likewise, Immersed in this feeling, kissing **Idhya**'s belly, trying to understand baby's soul, I gave blessings and sermons.

War was taking a severe form in the country, but my time was devoted to **Idhya**'s service, and I was being forgotten somewhere in her love. I jumped up and danced that day too, on which day our child also danced inside **Idhya**'s belly. I used to get more and more excited by the condition of **Idhya**, which was gradually changing into shape, I used to brought all the nutrients, medicine needed for **Idhya** from **Beni** market. It was my routine to lovingly kiss the love mark that grew on her belly. **Idhya** used to say "don't be too much, fortune also sometimes become greedy and give the curse." and I used to reply "I have seen many things with our children, This sign of our love is the diviner of we two, I known, nothing will happen". She *used to hug me even with some strain.*

CHAPTER ELEVEN

The beginning

*Rumors started to be heard in the village that red soldiers had made a camp near **Lukum** village and they were reaching it on foot from many places. **Posta** brother used to tell me that training and parades are going on in Lukum these days, they are giving training to kill people using sand sculptures. Many of the resources needed by that huge army were arranged from the surrounding villages, from food and vegetables to goats and wealth and weapons, they started arranging from the surrounding villages, everyone said. They even came to our village with guns, **Madal** and **sarangi**, to take whatever they get in the village. On the same day, after finishing dancing and singing, they also ordered that Villagers are not allowed to go to **Beni** market. I was very scared by that news because the day our child would see this world was today or tomorrow and in case of difficulty I had no other option except taking **Idhya** to **Beni** for delivery. When I said in a panicked voice that*

*"**Beni** barrack is going to end", **Idhya** held my hand and said "Don't be afraid, I don't have to go to **Beni** for delivery, I am strong enough".*

*"It's rumor, **Mabadi** left **Lukum** and arrived to **Takam** by walking" said one of the loquacious person gathering at **Chautara** as if he only had the intelligence and information. Again the other said, "Let's not say **Mabadi**, all the people are waking up with them, but don't know, when the people over here are going to wake up?" However, the support given by the people in that revolution could be heard. The battalions of the People's Liberation Army advancing towards **Beni** were not only provided with food and accommodation in the villages, but the people of the villages joined the front and were coming towards **Beni**.*

*"**Prakash** brother, sister-in-law is panicking alot" I listened this voice who was lost in the rhythm of gossip but I could not hold myself by this voice and reached home in a hurry. By the time I reached home, some women of the village had already arrived. Someone was consoling, "Don't worry, it's like normal this time." At such a time, I should stay with **Idhya***

*but they mocked me and not even allowed me to meet her. I stayed outside for a long time wishing for the good health of **Idhya** and the child. My heart was so scared without hearing **Idhya**'s voice, even after hours passed and there was no sound coming, my anxiety increased. I was made a fool, **Idhya** was soo panicked and completely unconscious. As soon as I understood **Idhya**'s condition, I got angry with everyone and moved towards **Beni** to bring the doctor. Even when my mother reminded me that "There is a lot of **mabadi** troops everywhere, even they told not to go towards **Beni,** if you suspect, you will be blown away, don't go anywhere." Even when my mother reminded me, I did not obey and I walked without paying attention to the darkness of the night. While walking at that time of the night, I saw a huge group of people on the way, there were young, old and women in that group, most of them looked like they hadn't bathed from long time. Later I came to know that the crowd was of the people's liberation army, which was going to separate and travel towards **Kushma, Baglung, Ghumaune Tal, Paribeni** one by one. However, for the sake of **Idhya**, I went forward without fear. When I found myself alone at night, I fell under their suspicion, they pointed a gun at me, but after I held my own, they lowered the gun and began to interrogate me. I told them the whole story. "You cannot go to **Beni** in the present situation, go back to your home, we will not let you go. A team of ours will* *be stationed in this village as well, that team will help you, now go back home!" Afraid to see such a large group of people, I had to helplessly accept their comfort and return home.*

*That night became the most painful night of my life, my eyes could not hold back tears seeing that condition of **Idhya**, there was no enthusiasm on anyone's face, everyone had lost. I was shaking her hands and feet, splashing water, shouting to bring her back to her senses. At that time, a group of red soldiers women arrived, they came with some medicine and injections. They told everyone to go out and closed the door. "Revolutionaries are not like the pictures we make in our minds, they are also human beings," I continued to think sitting in Balcony. Frontage **Darwang** village was also bustling that night.*

CHAPTER TWELVE

Beni Attack

The morning of the next day, illuminated by the bright sun of March , signaled a good day, **Idhya***'s senses also opened in the morning, and then my panicked mind got some peace. The revolutionaries also appear only at night like firefly, very skillful. In contrast to the situation at night, the atmosphere of the silence during the day and the imprisoned villagers could not give information to the royal soldiers who were sitting in barracks eating government rice. Even though the revolutionaries entered the houses, the villages were calm that day. After hearing that there is a big attack on Beni in the next three days, none of the villagers came out of their houses. In that atmosphere of emptiness, I was terrified,* **Idhya** *was shaking with pain from the moment she opened her senses, she was screaming, she was bawling. The pain she got sometimes hurt me as if I had been hurt. On that day, the pain of childbirth did not leave her, I was terrified, I called all the gods and goddesses on that day, "O God,* be good", I vowed to Goddess **Bhagwati**, "O Goddess, protect us". I also sincerely apologized to **Idhya**, "Sorry! Even if you want to, I will never let you fall into this type of pain again!" I also prayed to the women soldiers of the Red Army who gave me good hope, "Save my life". In this way, I had to suffer the same pain again and again for the whole day.

After the late evening, the groups of liberation army again started appearing all over the village. Around ten o'clock in the night, a loud noise suddenly spread in the environment from **Darwang**. Scared by the sound of guns and explosive bombs, everyone went to hide inside the house, the birds that had already settled in the nest started rounding in the sky began to show signs of great crisis. The revolutionaries started the attack by setting positions in the windows of the houses and offices of **Beni Bazar**. The sound of gunfire was heard for a long time from **Mangalghat** market, the royal army also retaliated with large bombs, with that bombing, fire spread to the entire eastern hill. **Beni's** prison was also attacked, all the prisoners were freed and the prison was destroyed. Houses, offices and shops in the market were also seen burning, screams of women and children were heard up to our village. On the other hand, our child, who did not witness that great battle, was still struggling like hell to come to this horrible world, **Idhya**'s struggle was the same. No one slept that night, everyone was wishing for "the end of that time, everyone's safety". Bombs were raining, guns were bursting, the sound of screams was echoing everywhere but after some hours of cacophony, that situation gradually became normal with less sounds. After two or three o'clock in the morning, nothingness won and I went up to balcony and became a witness of that time. The birds were moving in the sky as same like before, there was silence everywhere. Just then, a voice broke the silence. That sound was **Idhya**'s pain, she started screaming louder than yesterday, causing an earthquake in my heart. No matter how fierce the conflict that started from, silence win at the end, the finality of the end is true, I felt like, **Idhya**'s pain was also at its peak, so, peace prevailed everywhere. After a while, my ears were filled with the sound of a baby crying. The gift given to me by **Idhya** after a great struggle, "our child" was born.

CHAPTER THIRTEEN

Fire to burn myself

*The next day, helicopters appeared in the sky of **Beni Bazar**, which had been captured by the revolutionaries. After that, there was a tense situation like the whole day in **Beni Bazaar** and surrounding areas. The attack and weapons were transported by helicopter, the revolutionaries left the market the next day, but the attack continued. Thus, the **Beni Bazaar** that I have seen since my childhood, the **Beni Bazaar** with such a long history, the **Beni Bazaar** that is connected to every part of my life, was destroyed in a few days, the beautiful buildings of the **Beni Bazaar** were destroyed, the black smoke of the fire continued to fly from place to place for a few days. Bullets were visible in the shed of **Beni**, where the pilgrims were to meet, there was a big clash in barrack "Lots of people lost a lot." Various temples of **Beni** have also been destroyed, "God has also been destroyed, there is no God anymore, the **Kaliyug** has covered it," mother used to say. This beautiful world created by God is being* *destroyed by humans even now. After that incident, the village was deserted, many people fled. I still see the pain of the youths of my generation who left their villages in the war for the country and the youths who are going abroad for the country nowdays as the same.*

I have fallen many times while playing in that playground of confluence, but I was very emotional when I saw the bodies of policemen, rebels and common people who were in eternal peace without being able to get up in that same playground. Then I remembered my friend **Sonam** *too. I was worried thinking that "all those who die are the children of Nepali mothers". After our child was born, I realized that the source of life is nothingness and the end is also nothingness. In fact, we who cry till the end of our lives do not try to understand that riddle of nothingness. The God we believe is situated in that nothingness from which both creation and end occur. To take in God is to take in nothingness. All those martyrs were to be taken to eternal peaceful emptiness, all of them were freed from the pain of worldliness, born around* **Kaligandaki,** *after experiencing life around here, everyone's life flew away as smoke in the belly of* **Kaligandaki.**

I am sticking to my promise to you **Idhya**, *I will not belong to anyone except you for the rest of my life. I will collect every memory of every moment you have given me since childhood. I will not leave this village because you are with me everywhere in common well, in* **Deurali**, *in the forest of rhododendron, in the fields. Every moment you have given me is a gift for me, so I will live with the dead soul in your memory by remebering over the gifts yo gave me.*

Idhya *and the mother Nepal, who were overwhelmed by the pain of childbirth, felt the same pain that day and I thought to the mother Nepal in my mind, "Be patient, mother, your pain will end soon, peace will be born soon, you should not die, mother, you should not be a martyr." May the doctor and the cure meet soon, may the war won't kill you as it kills my love.*

Freed from all pain, drowned in the depths of peace, I had given a holy fire to my beloved **Idhya**, *who was sleeping on the bed of the pyre with a faint sigh. That day, I felt like, I set fire* *to my own life, myself.*

"Dad, why are you looking at the sky? Why did you throw away the tweezers and the mirror?"

*"My son, there is an ocean of gifts in the depth of the sky, you see, that vast sky has become narrow with the gifts given by **Idhya**, there are streams of gift there, I am looking those streams of gift."*

Lorose
- Bibek Aarunya Kafle

Beautiful Beni Market Nowdays

A story is a flowing river, its destination is the ocean. There is no end to the story, it is the ocean itself.

Bibek Aarunya Kafle, May 21 ,2000, ,
bibekaarunya@gmail.com, +977 9869111072/ +977
9869111073, Nepal